D0113954

Dear Parent:

Congratulations! Your child is taking the first steps on an exciting journey. The destination? Independent reading!

STEP INTO READING® will help your child get there. The program offers five steps to reading success. Each step includes fun stories and colorful art. There are also Step into Reading Sticker Books, Step into Reading Math Readers, Step into Reading Phonics Readers, Step into Reading Write-In Readers, and Step into Reading Phonics Boxed Sets—a complete literacy program with something to interest every child.

Learning to Read, Step by Step!

Ready to Read   Preschool–Kindergarten
• big type and easy words • rhyme and rhythm • picture clues
For children who know the alphabet and are eager to begin reading.

Reading with Help   Preschool–Grade 1
• basic vocabulary • short sentences • simple stories
For children who recognize familiar words and sound out new words with help.

Reading on Your Own   Grades 1–3
• engaging characters • easy-to-follow plots • popular topics
For children who are ready to read on their own.

Reading Paragraphs   Grades 2–3
• challenging vocabulary • short paragraphs • exciting stories
For newly independent readers who read simple sentences with confidence.

Ready for Chapters   Grades 2–4
• chapters • longer paragraphs • full-color art
For children who want to take the plunge into chapter books but still like colorful pictures.

STEP INTO READING® is designed to give every child a successful reading experience. The grade levels are only guides. Children can progress through the steps at their own speed, developing confidence in their reading, no matter what their grade.

Remember, a lifetime love of reading starts with a single step!

For Elle, who stole our hearts

Step into Reading, Random House, and the Random House colophon are registered trademarks of Random House, Inc.

Visit us on the Web!
StepIntoReading.com
randomhouse.com/kids
myprettypenny.com

Educators and librarians, for a variety of teaching tools, visit us at
randomhouse.com/teachers

Library of Congress Cataloging-in-Publication Data
Kinch, Devon.
Pretty Penny comes up short / by Devon Kinch. — 1st ed.
    p. cm.
Summary: Penny and her friends set up a drive-in movie theater to raise funds to buy feed for Doodle's Animal Farm, but Iggy the pig decides that some of the profits should be for him.
ISBN 978-0-375-86978-5 (trade) — ISBN 978-0-375-96978-2 (lib. bdg.) —
ISBN 978-0-375-98544-7 (ebook)
1. Fund raising—Fiction. 2. Stealing—Fiction. 3. Motion picture theaters—Fiction. 4. Pigs—Fiction. I. Title.
PZ7.K5653 Pk 2012 [E]—dc22 2010053949

Printed in the United States of America

10 9 8 7 6 5 4 3 2 1

Pretty Penny
Comes Up Short

By Devon Kinch

Random House 🏠 New York

It is a sunny summer day.
Penny and Iggy are
playing outside.
Penny is trying to beat Iggy
at hopscotch.
Iggy always wins.

Here comes Buck.

He lives on the third floor.

"Hi, Buck," says Penny.

"What are you up to?"

"Hi, Penny," says Buck.

"I am hanging up flyers."

Buck hands Penny a flyer
for Doodle's Animal Farm.
He volunteers there.
The farm has horses,
sheep, dogs, cows, and pigs.
"Doodle's Animal Farm
needs money," explains Buck.
"Every cent donated helps them
feed the animals."

baa the Sheep

Doodle's
ANIMAL FARM
→ needs your support ←

Coco the Cow

DONATIONS
NEEDED!

Help Doodle's Animal Farm raise money to feed and care for the animals. Donations are needed and volunteers are welcome!

Visit us at 33 Doodle Bean Way

Peggy & Sid the Pigs

Penny would like to donate money.

She loves animals.

Iggy does, too.

Pigs are his favorite!

Penny digs in her purse.

She has exactly zero dollars

and zero cents.

How can they help out?

Up in her room,

Penny checks her Saving Setup.

She counts $5.50 in her sharing jar.

This is money she has saved

to give to others in need.

She will donate this money

to Doodle's Animal Farm.

But she wants to do more!

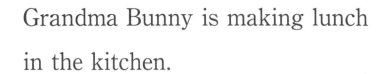

Grandma Bunny is making lunch
in the kitchen.
Penny tells her about the farm.
"I need a big idea to raise money!"
explains Penny.
"How about a penny drive?"
says Bunny.

"No, something much bigger,"
Penny says.
"A lemonade stand?"
says Bunny.
"Even bigger!" Penny says.

"I've got it!" yells Penny.

"We will open a movie theater!

A drive-in movie theater!"

Penny sketches it out on paper.

"That *is* pretty big," Bunny says.

Penny is going to need help.

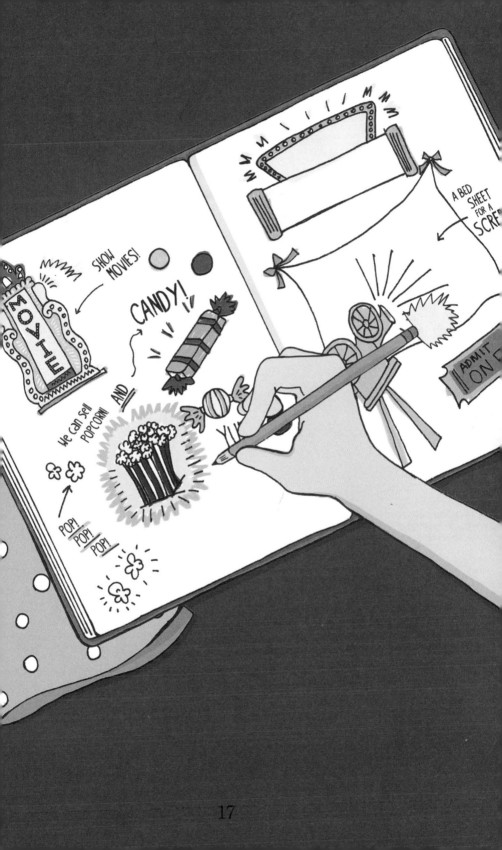

Penny runs upstairs and knocks
on Emma's door.
Emma and Maggie answer it.
Penny tells the girls
all about her big idea.
"We will help!" they say.
"We need a plan,"
says Penny.
They are all excited
about helping the animals.

They head upstairs

to the Small Mall

for a team meeting.

Everyone gets a job to do.

Maggie will make the signs.

She finds markers and

poster board.

Emma will be the usher.
She finds just the right outfit
for the job!

Penny will run the projector.

Iggy will run the snack stand.

He heads down to the kitchen.

It is his favorite room!

Bunny helps him pop popcorn.

He cannot resist sneaking some.

It is opening night at

Penny's Drive-In Movie Theater.

All the chairs are in place.

The popcorn has been popped.

The team is ready.

"Come one, come all!"

shouts Penny.

"All money will be donated to

Doodle's Animal Farm!"

First the Wilsons arrive.

Then Miss Piper and her friend
come on roller skates.

Buck shows up on his skateboard.

Soon everyone

from the neighborhood

rolls in on a set of wheels.

The snack stand is a hit!
Iggy has more customers
than he can handle.
Money starts to pile up
on the counter.
He puts some money
in the register.
But some money
falls on the ground.

Hot & Buttery
POPCORN
50¢

Gum balls
25¢

The movie is about to begin!

The snack line is still long.

Iggy is flustered.

He swipes the money

into his hat.

He pops the hat on his head.

"Shhh!" Emma whispers.

She pulls the curtains aside.

FILM NOIR CLASSIC

A Pretty Penny Production Film

IGGYBLANCA

Starring Penny & Iggy

Penny starts the movie.

Everyone is having a great time.

They blow bubbles and

munch popcorn.

Iggy watches the movie.

He's careful not to jingle

the money.

He decides to keep the money

in his hat for himself.

The money is for animals.

Iggy *is* a pig.

He likes food, too.

He daydreams about the treats

he will buy.

It all seems fair to him.

The movie is over,

and everyone rolls home.

"We earned twenty-six dollars

from tickets!"

Penny cheers.

"How much money did we earn

from the snack stand?"

she asks.

Iggy shrugs.

The girls add up the money.

The grand total is $29.50!

The next day

everyone meets outside.

They are going

to Doodle's Animal Farm.

They cannot wait

to donate the money!

Everyone feels proud.

On the way there
Iggy stops to buy treats.
First, at the candy store
for a lollipop.

Then at the ice cream shop.

Then at a hot dog cart.

Penny is curious.

"Where did you get the money
for this?" asks Penny.

Iggy's mouth is full of treats.

Penny puts her hands on her hips
and waits.

"Iggy!" she says.

He takes off his hat.

Money falls on the ground.

"This money is not for you,

Iggy," she explains.

"We earned this money

for the farm animals.

You cannot take

what does not belong to you."

"That's stealing!" says Emma.

Penny tells Iggy

he will have to earn back

every cent.

She takes away his hot dog.

Penny's team arrives at the farm.

Emma says that they would

like to make a donation.

"Thank you!" says Buck.

Buck explains that they are also

looking for volunteers today.

They need help cleaning out

the animal pens.

Penny gets another big idea.

She knows the perfect pig
who can volunteer.
Iggy is happy to help out.
He sure did learn his lesson.
One scoop at a time!